The Water Park

by Michèle Dufresne
Illustrations by Sterling Lamet

Literacy Footprints, Inc.

"Come here, Georgie," said Father Giraffe.
"Come here, Little Dinosaur.
Come here, Baby Stegosaurus.
Here is a water slide!"

3

Look at Georgie.
Georgie is going down the water slide.

Look at Little Dinosaur.
Little Dinosaur is going down the water slide.
Look at Monkey.
Monkey is going down the water slide, too. 5

"Come here, Baby Stegosaurus. Come here!" said Father Giraffe.

"No," said Baby Stegosaurus.
"No!"

"Come here, Baby Stegosaurus.
Come here!"

"No," said Baby Stegosaurus.
"The water slide is too big!"

"Look," said Father Giraffe.
"Here is a **little** water slide!"

Georgie is going down the water slide.
Little Dinosaur is going down the water slide.
Monkey is going down the water slide.

Baby Stegosaurus is going down
a water slide, too.